ATTENTION READERS: We would like to hear what you think about our books. Please send your comments or suggestions to:

Signal Hill Publications
P.O. Box 131
Syracuse, NY 13210-0131

• • •

SIGNAL HILL™
PUBLICATIONS
Copyright © 1991
Signal Hill Publications
An imprint of New Readers Press
U.S. Publishing Division of Laubach Literacy International
Box 131, Syracuse, New York 13210-0131

10 9 8 7 6 5 4 3 2

First printing: March 1991

ISBN 1-929631-37-4

The words "Writers' Voices" are a trademark of Signal Hill Publications.

Cover designed by Paul Davis Studio
Interior designed by Barbara Huntley

The articles in this book were edited with the cooperation and consent of the authors. Every effort has been made to locate the copyright owners of material reproduced in this book. Omissions brought to our attention will be corrected in subsequent editions.

Acknowledgments

We gratefully acknowledge the generous support of the following foundations and corporations that made the publication of WRITERS' VOICES and NEW WRITERS' VOICES possible: An anonymous foundation; The Vincent Astor Foundation; Booth Ferris Foundation; Exxon Corporation; James Money Management, Inc.; Knight Foundation; Philip Morris Companies Inc.; Scripps Howard Foundation; The House of Seagram and H.W. Wilson Foundation.

We would also like to thank the following tutors whose dedicated work with our student authors has enhanced our book: Ellen Abrams, Liz Fiske, Marion Greenstone, Lori Gum, Michelle Laney, Emma LaPrince, Gary Murphy, Robin Power, Kathleen Quintana, Ann Silver, Beverly Smith, and Larry Williams.

For their hard work and enthusiastic participation, we would like to thank our student authors. Special thanks to Mrs. Beulah Martin.

Our thanks to Paul Davis Studio and Myrna Davis, Paul Davis, Jeanine Esposito, Alex Ginns and Frank Begrowicz for their inspired design of the covers of these books. Thanks also to Barbara Huntley for her sensitive design of the interior of this book and to Ron Bel Bruno for his timely help.

Tower Hamlets

Suppliers Code	AVA
Price	£2.95
Invoice Date	01/11/2006
LOC	BET
Class	428.6
Barcode	C001278653

Tower Hamlets

CONTENTS

INTRODUCTION

There are many ways to take charge of your life. You can change your job, your friends, your home, your habits . . . even your point of view.

Each of the authors of these stories and poems took charge of his or her own life in one way or another. For example, the writers of "A New World" and "Walking a Straight Line" each moved to a new place to improve their lives—one from a different country to the United States and one from a small southern town to New York City. In "Jake and I" and "You Never Know," the writers describe their struggles to control their addictions.

Sometimes we take charge by changing the way we think about ourselves. In "Choosing Sides," the writer defines his cultural and racial identity; in "New Thoughts About My Life," the author rewrites her past and uses her happy memories to brighten her present life.

As you read these pieces, you might put yourself in the place of the writers. How would you have handled the situation? What would you have done differently?

You will probably be reminded of the times you have taken charge of your own life. And you may also think about parts of your life that you want to be more fully in charge of. You may remember the frustration as well as the satisfaction you felt in taking charge of a situation you faced. And we hope you will also reflect on the courage both you and the authors in this book showed in taking charge of life.

— Ann Heininger, Staff Member
Literacy Volunteers of New York City

FAKING IT

Anonymous

It's amazing what a person can do by bluffing. Looking back, it seems like all my working life I was faking it. . . .

I needed a job. A friend of mine told me about a place that was hiring truck drivers. I had never driven a truck in my life—in fact, I'd just gotten my driver's license. I walked to the office to apply for the job.

When I went in, the receptionist gave me an application and said, "Fill this out." I asked her, "Do you mind if I take this out to my car?" She said, "No, go right ahead." I didn't have a car but she didn't know that! I ran all the way home and had my sister fill out the application for me.

I ran back and gave the application to the receptionist. She looked at it and said, "Okay, we'll give you an interview."

I talked to the owner. I told him I had no experience driving a truck but I would like to give it a try. He hired me but I didn't let him know that I couldn't read.

In the beginning, I made local stops around the city. When we loaded the truck in the morning, they gave me a bill of lading. It listed the customers' names and addresses and the merchandise each one was to get. I knew the letters in the alphabet, so I matched the letters on the packages to the letters on the bill of lading. I knew that if I saw ten items on the bill of lading, I had to give the customer ten packages. I got away with it!

My boss came to me and said, "We're going to give you the Jersey stops." This consisted of 30 to 40 stops a day with over 300 packages.

Every day, the first thing I did when I got to Jersey was look for a cop. When I saw one, I would show him my bill of lading and ask if he could give me directions to the address. The cop would tell me it was two miles up the street, make a right or whatever, and what the name of the customer was. When I got there, I'd match up the first name on the bill of lading with the packages and deliver them. Then I'd look for another cop. I'd ask him for directions to the next stop. I wouldn't tell him the name of the customer because I didn't know it—but he would tell me. Again, I got away with it!

And that's how it went for four or five years. I became a very good delivery man without anyone knowing that I couldn't read.

One day a friend of mine told me about another job. I said, "Well, it's paying more than I'm making. Okay, bring me the application and let me fill it out—that way, I'll save some time." So he brought me the application and I had my sister fill it out. I went for an interview and they hired me.

Much to my amazement, I was very handy with the machines in the factory. I learned right away. I worked myself up to lead man. One day the boss came to me and said, "We want you to be foreman." The pay was so good that I had to take a shot at it. When he asked if I could handle it, I said, "Sure I can!"

This happened on a Thursday and payday was Friday. The boss gave me the checks to hand out. "Oh, wow," I thought, "now what am I going to do?" I had a friend working there. I said to him, "Bob, I'm going to give you a responsibility. I'm very busy right now, so I want you to hand out these checks for me." He was happy to do it.

I knew I had to learn those names. But there were 20 employees under me. When I got home, I told my sister every person's name. She wrote them down and I started memorizing them.

The next payday, I handed out the checks. No one ever guessed that I'd just memorized the guys' names. Nobody ever knew that I couldn't read.

As foreman, I had to meet with customers over lunch or dinner. I thought "uh-oh" the first time I had to take out a customer. We were going to a high-class restaurant. I asked myself, "What do I do when I get the menu?"

When the waitress gave me the menu, I put it in front of me like I was reading it. I thought, "This is a high-class place, they've got to have filet mignon steak." So I told the waitress, "I'll have the filet mignon." She said, "Rare, medium or well-done?" That part was easy. I said, "Medium."

Later, I found out about Literacy Volunteers of New York City. That's when I got my chance to learn to read. I didn't think I'd learn. I really didn't. The sounds, the vowels—nothing came easily. But I kept on pushing and now I can read. I'm no longer faking it.

WALKING A STRAIGHT LINE: A WORKING LIFE

Marvita Spann

I came to New York City from the South in February 1946. At the time, New York was the cleanest, most beautiful place I had ever seen. A newspaper was 2 cents, the bus fare was 5 cents and my three-room apartment cost $12 a month. I got a job at the Sunshine Biscuit factory. The pay was $12.50 a week.

Everything seemed magical back then, even the place I worked. It was amazing just to see all the cookies that came out of that factory—Krispy crackers, Chip-A-Roos, Vanilla Wafers. There must have been 50 kinds. And the building itself was huge: nine floors high with a thousand windows. Everything that was used to package the biscuits was made right there—even the paper and the glue.

The biscuit factory was a wonderful place to work. I met all kinds of people there. We would laugh and talk about how we were raised up; we would talk about our families and friends.

Of course, it wasn't always easy to work with a lot of people you didn't know. Some liked you, some were jealous of you and some would try to get you fired.

There was also some tension between whites and blacks. I don't think my supervisor liked working with blacks at first but she had no choice. The company had just started to hire blacks during World War II. Eventually, we got used to each other—we even became friends.

My supervisor used to wonder how I learned to do the work so fast. It went back to my days on the farm. I came from the country—a little place called Kings Mountain, North Carolina. My mother used to take us to work in the fields where they grew cotton. I picked and hoed it. I could just watch someone do something once and I picked it up right away.

As years went by, I learned more about the people I worked with. There was a lot of jealousy. Sometimes it seemed that almost every day you were in the office, looking at the plant manager, explaining your way out of something someone said you did. It kept me praying all the time but it made me a better worker.

I remember one morning when there were five of us on the animal-cookie machine. We each had a different job. The foreman told us to start the machine. We were talking and moving too slow, so he fired us all. We went to the shop steward right away but we still had to go home. Three of the five went to the racetrack. They made more money at the track than they would have made working. I was playing numbers at the time, so I went home and played my number. It came out. I also made more money than I would have at work. We all went back to work the next morning but we had to walk a straight line for a while.

We used to get paid on Thursday. Some workers would go out to cash their checks and come back with beer and whiskey. All the drinkers would have some. It would get so bad, the cookies would go all over the place.

Once a supervisor found a six-pack of beer in my group. The next day, we all had to go see the plant manager. I used to be a drinker, but by that time I had given it up. I was not the guilty one and they knew it. We all knew who brought in the liquor, but no one would tell. After that, security got really tight in the plant. A year later, they started paying us in cash so no employee would have to go out.

We had a cooling system above the conveyor belt so that by the time the cookies reached us in packing, they wouldn't be so hot. Many of us wore gloves. Otherwise, we would have gotten blisters on our fingers.

Sometimes the cooling system would break down or they would forget to turn it on. The union president would walk onto the factory floor and say, "Stop the machines. These biscuits are too hot for my workers." We had a strong union. The president really protected our rights.

In 1955, we went on strike for about six weeks. I enjoyed myself; I went all over. I went to the movies, to the beach. Without the union, they could have fired us all.

When the biscuit company moved to New Jersey, I went with them. Things were different. The New Jersey factory was all on one floor—you could walk for three miles in that factory!

As years went by, they got automatic machines. All you had to do was push a button and watch the work pack itself. A conveyor belt would take the cookies through packing, down to shipping and onto the truck.

Another thing that changed along the way was the division between men's and women's work. It used to be that men were the only ones who could run the machines. The women packed and bundled. Of course men got paid more for their work. As the years passed, women learned to run the machines. Some of them did it better than the men. Women tended to keep things cleaner.

You would think that discrimination would have ended by the time we moved to New Jersey. It sometimes seemed like it was just beginning. Now there were Spanish and Indian and Chinese people working at the factory, too. Those white people did not like to be told what to do. It took some time but it got worked out.

When I retired in 1986, they gave me a lovely party. I got a beautiful watch and other nice gifts. The president of the company had a luncheon for me. They didn't want me to retire but after 40 years, I was ready to rest. Now I go back once a year to see my friends.

THOUGHTS ABOUT LIFE

Anthony Harris

A MAN

To be a man is a way of life. Some do not have time to be what they can be. They only have time to be.

I have often thought about the importance of having a powerful plan in life. Why a plan? Because a man must have a beat to dance to. The show must go on but will the man go on the show?

Men will never know their purpose on earth. But a man should know the purpose of being a man.

Life is not responsible for me.
I am responsible for life.

BLACK REALITY

To be black is to be strong
In being black, there is nothing wrong
To be black, it's an honor
Like looking into the night
   and seeing a knight in shining armor

I am black from the color of my skin
There's a body with nothin' sorry
Black is a color that will never change
Within this color, there lies more than
   just a name
A human being
With every emotion there could ever be

I feel no shadow within my heart
But I've met the shadow that blocks the dark
No shadow will ever block my thought

LIFE WITH NO SOUND
(Thinking About Someone Who
Cannot Hear Me)

Life is like sound
Sound travels
But often sound is not heard
Sound always looks for a hungry ear
   that cares and has the ability
   to respond
When I say sound, I say life
Expression is the voice in a silent life
A man or woman who cannot hear
   has the sound of life
That sound can usually be heard by eyes
   that love to listen

The next time you see a life
   that has no sound
Listen with your eyes
And you will hear life passing by

PROJECT LIFE

Rats   Mice   Too many worries
Men at peace
   when their bodies are <u>buried</u>

The projects are another form
   of death camp
Children raped in the depths
   of a cellar ramp

Muggin' and no lovin'
Frightening drug wars on every floor
A noise wakes me up
   in the midnight hour
a bullet shower
over power
to rule the turf
Perhaps there's a drug lord

This is the chaos of the projects
Darkness and light
One life taken
One given back at birth
I'm thinkin' positive
Project life

CAT HAS HER DREAM

Mamie Moore

April 7th: Yesterday my daughter Catherine gave birth to her dream—a baby girl. When it was all over, we wrote this birth journal. It's one story me, my daughter and my grandchildren can read together.

10:00 A.M.: Cat and I go to the clinic. The doctor tells Cat she is fine. He says, go home and relax. If she sees telltale signs, go to the hospital.

5:00 P.M.: Cat tells me she is starting to have some pain. She has to go to the bathroom. I say, no, you cannot go! She asks, why, Mom? I say, if you do that, the baby might come out in the toilet. Hee, hee, we laugh. I say, let's go to the hospital. Cat says, no, let me eat first!

5:30 P.M.: Cat's eaten, thank God. All she thinks about is food. And the pain, which is starting to get worse. I call 911. They send a cop named Mike. I say to Cat, why, what a hunk.

24

6:00 P.M.: Mike calls the ambulance. We wait about 20 minutes before he calls again. Mike says, are you her mother? I say yes. He says, you look like her sister. Then he says to Cat, it's not that you look old, it's just that your mother looks young. That makes me feel real good.

6:30 P.M.: The ambulance comes. Cat and I get into it.

6:45 P.M.: We arrive at the hospital and the doctor examines Cat. He tells us to go walk in the hallway; the baby needs to be walked down. Boy, you sure see a lot of funny people while waiting for a baby to be born.

8:00 P.M.: The pains are about six minutes apart. Laughing at Cat, I say, boy, you sure are ugly. Cat says, Mom, please don't make me laugh.

9:00 P.M.: The pains are three minutes apart. Every time Cat gets a pain, we can see the baby move down. I've never seen anything like it before.

9:30 P.M.: The doctor sees Cat again. He says everything is all right, you have about two hours to go. The doctor tells me to get

Cat a soda. He doesn't want Cat to get dehydrated.

10:45 P.M.: Cat wants ice. She asks me to get it. I say no. The ice is a long way down the hall. I tell her my leg is hurting. Cat says, Mama, I'll go get it. When she gets up, a big pain hits her. Cat takes about six steps and another big pain hits her. Cat says, oh Mama, it hurts. It's the first time she's cried out. I know it's almost time for the baby to come. Cat can't move.

10:55 P.M.: Cat is in the hallway bent all the way down. She has her "bloody show" and is bearing down. I know if I don't get her to the delivery room fast, my second grandchild will be born on the floor. So I grab her dress and tell her not to push. I'm scared that if I let go of her dress, the baby will fall on the floor. I finally get up enough nerve to go get a nurse. The nurse just stands there and yells, what is she doing down there? I say, she is about to have the baby. The nurse is mad. So am I. While the nurse stands there not helping, Cat is crying and holding her legs together. I think of ways to get that nasty nurse.

11:00 P.M.: Another nurse comes with a wheelchair and takes Cat into the delivery room.

11:15 P.M.: The nurse comes out and says, it's a girl. I say, oh, thank you, God. I was so happy because we did not want a boy. Boys are so bad.

11:30 P.M.: The nurse brings my daughter out so I can see her and the baby girl. Cat tells me the baby's name is Keywana. She weighs 8 pounds 9 ounces.

MIDNIGHT: I go home and dream about my new grandchild.

GOD HAS BEEN GOOD TO ME

Anonymous

I was born in New York City in 1964. When I was very young, my mother and father separated. I lived with my mother but I stayed close to my father. He always spoiled me because I was the baby of the family. I always wanted my parents to get back together.

I started going to school when I was four years old. I didn't like it. I would cry when I had to go to school.

When I was in junior high, I started playing hookey. I would spend the day at my friend's house. At three o'clock I would go home and pretend to do homework.

By the time I got to high school, I was playing hookey every day and going to hookey parties. The school called my father every day because of it. He would drive around the neighborhood looking for me. He finally got me to go back to school.

But I got in with a bad crowd. I started

getting high on drugs and I sold drugs, too. I was going downhill.

When my father found out I was on drugs, he said I had to stay in the house for a year and I couldn't go to school. That last part made me happy.

By the time the year was over, I was 18. I started hanging around with the wrong people and getting high again.

I met a man named Mark. He was a year younger than me. We started talking and going to the movies and out to dinner. Then Mark and I moved in with my sister. I got pregnant. We had a baby girl named Marie.

Finally Mark and I got our own apartment. We were together for four years, but then Mark went to jail. I cried for him.

Marie and I moved in with my cousin Roz. After a year, we moved in with my close friend Cindy.

Soon I met Anthony. We started talking and going out to different places. Anthony moved in with Cindy and me. But a year later, we broke up. Anthony started seeing Cindy. When he moved in with her, Marie and I went back to my mother's. Life goes on.

I got a job in a shop. And I started going to school to learn how to read. The first day, I was very nervous. But after a week, I started to feel better about the school. Everyone was very nice to me.

Why did I go back when I used to hate school? One day Marie asked me to read a book to her. I told her to ask Grand-mommy. But I wanted to learn to read so I could read to her myself.

I made a friend, Pam, at the school. She always stopped at the cafeteria to get a soda on the way to school. She met John at the cafeteria. Pam thought I would like John so she introduced us. We started talking and dating.

John is all right with me. Marie likes him, too. I want God to bless our being together. I call John every day at his job just to hear his voice. I miss him when we are apart.

My cousin Roz came to my house one Sunday after church. She said God had sent her to me. I got saved that Sunday.

Every Tuesday Roz and I go to bible class. On Sundays Marie and I meet her at church. Even my mother started going to church with me and that has made me very happy.

I told Roz about John. She said to put myself in God's hands. She said if God wanted John and me to be together, he would bless us. And we will know that we are being blessed.

I asked John to come to church with me. He hasn't come yet. But God has been good to me. I am off drugs and learning to read and write. And when Marie went to kindergarten, she said to me, "Mommy, I'm a big girl now because I'm going to school just like you."

JAKE AND I

Eugene Jackson

On July 9, 1989, a good friend of mine died. He was in the hospital for a week before he died. I don't think his death surprised anyone.

We grew up together. We played together. He was my buddy and I was his. He was someone I could talk to. If you ever had a good friend who you could tell anything to, you know what I am talking about.

Jake and I started drinking together in 1956; we were 14. It was a lot of fun back then when we were young and wild. We did a lot of crazy things together when we were drinking. Somewhere along the way we crossed the invisible line and became alcoholics. Then it wasn't fun anymore, but that didn't stop us. We kept drinking day after day for years to come, even after our fun turned into suffering and pain.

I asked God many times to take my life. I am sure Jake did too, even though we didn't talk about it. We kept pretending that everything was OK.

I even stopped looking in the mirror because when I did, I could see death. But that still didn't stop me. I just kept drinking and so did Jake, day after day.

Sometimes I would look at Jake and I would say, "When I get that bad, I'll stop." He probably said the same thing about me.

Sometimes we would talk about getting our lives together and going to detox, but it was just talk. We just sat there all day, every day, talking about the good times we had in the past. We never talked to each other about the pain we were feeling. Things might have been different if we were honest. But we just kept pretending that we were fine, when we were both slowly dying from drink.

Most alcoholics go through years of suffering and pain before death and peace finally come. That's a terrible way to live. I decided I didn't want to die like that. I tried to detox myself. I didn't go to the hospital. That was a mistake.

After three days, I went into DTs and I began to see things and hear voices. In my lifetime I have known fear but it was never like this. I was seeing demons and talking to God. It was like a battle between good and evil. You would think after all that, I would stop. Not me. I just kept pretending I was fine.

On September 21, 1984, I woke up from a drunk. I never felt so bad in all my life. I went to the bathroom to get myself together. It had been a long time since I looked in the mirror. I didn't recognize the person I saw. Alcohol had changed me. My eyes were red as red can be. My skin was dark and ashy. That's when I knew I had to do something about my drinking. But I still went out and got drunk that day.

The next morning, I went to the hospital for detox. The first three days I was miserable, but then I began to try to get my thoughts together. I began to think differently and said to myself, "Why am I living this way?" This was the beginning of my recovery.

I had to search my heart and my mind to find the answer. I knew this was not going to be easy. After thinking for a long time, I decided to go to a long-term program. That's where I began to change.

I thought a lot about why things were changing for me. The answer was that I was talking about myself more, and that was something I had never done before. I stayed in the program for three months. I talked about Eugene. I let people know who I was and where I'd been. I talked about my suffering and pain.

I felt good about the way things were going for me but I still didn't feel strong enough to go back to the streets. I entered a longer-term program and began making AA meetings. I knew I was in the right place.

Immediately people told me they would love me until I learned to love myself. I could identify with that. When I thought about it, I had really never loved Eugene. There were a number of things I didn't like about myself: I didn't like being shy, I didn't like being insecure, I didn't like having low self-esteem. When a person doesn't love himself, he takes the easy way out by committing suicide. I was too cowardly for a quick fix, so I was letting alcohol do the job for me slowly.

I stopped going to Jake's house so much. When I did, I felt sorry for him. For the first time in years, I could really see how much pain Jake was in. I really wanted to help Jake, but there was nothing I could do until Jake wanted help for himself.

For the next three years, good things happened to me. I enrolled in a job program and got into the custodian's union. My legal records got straightened out and I got a certificate of good conduct from the court.

But my buddy Jake slowly died from alcohol. There wasn't a lot of crying at Jake's funeral. I didn't understand at first. But when I think about it, I believe everyone was just happy that Jake was out of his suffering. Peace had finally come.

A NEW WORLD

Mamie Chow

When I first came to the United States, life was strange. Everything was new—the country, the language, the customs. I had to learn everything all over again.

I left China in 1948. My parents arranged it; they wanted what was best for me. China was in ruins after the war. There was no work. There wasn't even enough food for everyone.

In the old days, young girls in China had their marriages arranged by their parents. I had never said a word to my parents about men. My mother had me dress up for a photograph. I didn't know why she wanted the picture. I learned later that she had sent it to a Chinese man living in New York.

One morning my mother dressed me up to go to town. We walked back and forth in front of a store. The man from New York had come to China to see me. He and his friends were inside the store watching me. I guess he liked me. Two weeks later we got married.

About six months later, we left China. I was pregnant. The boat took two weeks to get to San Francisco, California. Then we took a plane to Newark, New Jersey. All the travel made me dizzy but I was happy to come to New York City. I could have a job and make a living for my family.

My only problem was that I didn't speak English—not even a word. At first, I would only go out with my husband.

Still, there was so much to see. Some buildings were tall, some buildings were low, some buildings were very old. The subways were old and creaky and had cane seats, but they were safe and only cost a nickel.

There was one bad thing about New York—it was so hot, we couldn't sleep at night. We had only one fan, so sometimes my husband would take a blanket to the park and stay the night there. Back then, people weren't afraid to be in the park or street at night. There wasn't much crime.

In 1954, my husband and I bought a laundry from people we knew. The price was $2500. We borrowed all of the money.

We were tricked. After we ran the business a few months, someone came to tell us that the city was going to tear down the building. We were shocked.

That happened a lot. New York buildings were too old so the city tore them down. People would lose their businesses. The city gave you six months' notice, but it would be hard to find a new place to rent. This really hurt the small business people. We were lucky to find a new store, and that one turned out OK.

I had three children. It was hard for us but the whole family helped make our business a success.

I would take my children to school before I opened the store. My husband would already be there working. I would check the laundry and take care of the customers. When my younger daughter got off school, she would work the towel-rolling machines or fold tablecloths. She would work and study at the same time. She was a good girl—she listened to her parents and did what we asked.

When my older daughter got off school, she would take care of her baby brother. She would play with him, bathe him and cook the family dinner. Later she would do her homework.

My husband and I worked late every day. I stood all day to do the laundry. I got tired and my feet hurt. Sometimes we got home at 12:30 A.M. That was my life for 30 years.

Now I'm retired and can do what I like. After so many years in this new country, I am finally working on my language skills. I am proud of how far I have come.

NEW THOUGHTS ABOUT MY LIFE

Laura Medina

MY CHILDHOOD AS I WOULD HAVE WANTED IT

I am 13 years old and going to school with my sister and brothers. I would have seven brothers and one sister. We would have a big house and I would have my own room and all the pretty clothes that girls love. I would go to dancing and singing classes two times a week. My brothers and I would play games together and have a good time.

We would grow up and get married and have good jobs and visit one another. When my mother and father came to visit, we would talk about my childhood and how good life had been to us. We would give thanks to God who has played a very important part in our lives. We would never have to worry about love because we would have love from both sides, mother and father.

That is the childhood I would have wanted. I'd have white roller skates and a mother who liked to skate with me. When we stopped skating, we would talk and eat and I would tell her how my day went in school and how much I would love to sing at the Apollo one day. And she would smile and say, "Go for it."

I never had this as a child but I can try to give it to my little one. It's how I would have wanted my own childhood to be.

IN MY BEDROOM

I am in my bedroom and looking at it. I turn it on. It makes me feel good. When I am sad or happy, I put it on. You can tap your feet or your hands to it. People say sometimes it can be too high up. But I feel differently about my stereo. It's my music box and I love it. I love to sing and that's why it could never be out of my reach. You pay your bills and rent; people shouldn't tell you how to listen to your music.

When I play hip hop, it's all right. When I play church music, it's all right. So don't stop me from playing it. It makes me feel like I've got money. I feel like I am in sync with life. I love music and it makes me feel free.

I sing because I love to express myself with words. So I sing what I feel and it always comes out so pretty to me. It makes me feel like I'm standing on a high place and singing to the world.

I love to dance. I don't dance as well as I might. But I move to the music and that's what makes me happy.

GRANDMA WAS THE BEST WOMAN IN THE WORLD

My grandma's name was Laura Medina. She was 99 years old when she died. My grandma was so sweet to me. Because of her, I think of life as being joyful and wonderful.

When she and I began our day, she would come and sit down beside me and tell me stories about her life in the old country, Puerto Rico. She would tell me how she and my grandfather became lovers. I can still remember the satisfied look on her face when she told me how my grandfather asked her to marry him. Because of her color, his side of the family did not want them to be married. But my grandfather loved her, and did not care about what his family wanted.

Grandma would make my day by sitting there and asking me to sing and dance for her. When I write about her, I feel so good inside; she had so much love to give and she gave it to everyone.

She would fix iced tea for me and my friends. They would ask me, "What is she saying, Laura?" And I would translate for her. She would ask everyone who came over if they cared to stay and eat. Everybody loved her cooking; she made good rice and beans.

I miss her so much, sometimes I cry when I talk about her. That's why I can say with a truly good heart that if I could name her all over again, I would call her Love.

MY OTHER GRANDMA, THE WORLD'S GREATEST COOK

My other grandma's name is Mrs. Pinkney, and she is the world's greatest cook. When you knock on her door, you can smell her cooking coming through it. She opens the door with an "Oh, what do you want?" If you'd never met her before, you'd think she was a mean lady. But once you got in, you'd see differently. She would sit you down at the table and start talking to you; you would forget your first impression.

Pies, cakes and desserts sit on the table. Just looking at them makes you imagine them melting in your mouth. This lady has a way with children. She talks and fusses over you. She makes you feel like eating everything: the best cakes, pies, chicken and corn bread you would ever taste in your life. My grandmother should have a restaurant. We would call it Grandma Susie's Restaurant.

So remember, young and old, be good to those you love and have here on earth, because grandmas are hard to find.

MY CHILD'S FATHER WHO ONCE PLAYED A VERY SPECIAL PART IN MY LIFE

My baby's father came over and we talked. I am happy that he came to see his son but I don't want to be misled by it. I am asking God for help to understand it. He has hurt me in the past with so much lying that I don't know if I am ready for his so-called love again. I am happy when I see him spending time with his son. It makes me and Jerome feel good to know that he still cares in his own way. But I want a real family, not someone who just wants to make love and then say goodbye.

Love plays a very important part in your life, but not when it's just in the bedroom. That's why I only want to be friends.

We women have to separate lust from love in our minds. That's why I want to wait until I find someone who loves me and Jerome for us, someone who doesn't just want to take his mother to bed. Someone who wants to love God and have a job and who can be there in good times and bad times. Someone who you can just lay down beside and say that it's been a hard day but coming home to you has made it all worthwhile.

That's my dream of a family. Who knows, maybe it's not real but I sure want to see for myself if it can happen.

CHOOSING SIDES

Tony Slaughter

I am a young man who is from two backgrounds. For me, that has never been a problem, so it surprised me that it was a problem for anybody else. It never crossed my mind that my parents were different; the outside world forced me to think about it.

People don't like the idea of a black man being married to a white woman. When my parents were together, they never made a big deal of it. I was raised not to see the color of a person's skin but the love and goodness in his or her heart. Now racial hate is so bad that people are saying I must choose to be one or the other. I'm told I can't be both black and white, and that's where the conflict comes in. I sometimes feel I must choose sides and I don't want to.

That's why I have decided not to call myself black or white. I enjoy both my cultures and I'm proud of them both.

YOU NEVER KNOW

Millie Mendez

My name is Milagros Mendez but everyone knows me as Millie. I am a nuyorican,* born in Brooklyn, 1957.

I am an ex-alcoholic, an ex-drug addict and also an ex-homeless person.

The story that you are about to read is all true. I wrote it to say to people with problems that with willpower, problems can be solved. I've learned that where there is a will, there is a way.

PART ONE: WHEN I BECAME AN ALCOHOLIC

My life started to go downhill when I married a man I didn't love, just to cover my gay life. I knew that my parents wouldn't understand or accept my lifestyle.

For a year, I lived in hell. My husband

*A Puerto Rican who is born in or has lived in the continental United States.

was not a bad person. But I was hurting him and making a fool of myself. I decided it was best to get a divorce.

A few years later, I gave it another try with another man but things didn't work out. When I left, I discovered I was two months pregnant. I gave birth to a beautiful girl. Once I had her, I knew I couldn't keep on being a closet case. When you hide your true self, you lose your true self. It was time for me to tell my mother about my life.

My mother stopped talking to me. I let my mother take my daughter. I didn't have a safe home for her, plus I was not a responsible person at the time. I decided that it was best for me to live my life away from the family. My mother moved to Puerto Rico with the baby.

Time passed. I couldn't stop thinking about how I was rejected. I started to hang out and to drink in my apartment with friends. I thought it would solve my problems but it backfired.

I was drinking every day after work. My friends and I would smoke more than 15 joints a night and we'd down a pool of liquor. I would drink liquor like it was soda.

Sometimes I didn't sleep at all. I went to work drunk and had a nice cold beer for lunch. I was drinking so much that my eyes were like tomatoes and my breath smelled like pure alcohol. People at work advised me to stop but I didn't listen. For me, liquor was my best friend; it was my companion in my sorrow.

As time passed, things got worse. I kept thinking about my problems and my family. When I thought about them, I would grab a nice cold beer and drink my brains out.

Two years later, I decided to quit on my own. My friends thought it was a joke. I went home and took every can and bottle that contained liquor and threw them in the garbage. Then I got away from all my friends. Every day I went home, ate and watched TV until I fell asleep. Each night for weeks, I'd hear someone knocking at my door, but I wouldn't open it. I knew it was my friends wanting to hang out. It was hard to quit, but there was no way I was going to take another beer in my hands. Little by little, I felt better.

I started to spend money on things I

enjoyed: fixing my apartment and going out dancing. My boss gave me a promotion. I even found a companion. Things were going really well for me.

For three years I enjoyed a good life. I had everything I wanted. But one day my lover started to change on me and moved out without giving a reason. In time I found out that I wasn't making enough money for her. That hurt me so much. I was afraid I might go back to drinking, but I stayed strong and kept living my life as if nothing had happened.

PART TWO: WHEN I BECAME HOMELESS

Things were going great for me again but, like people say, problems are never far away. In February 1985, I lost everything. I lost my dreams and half of my life.

One afternoon on my way home from work, I saw fire engines in front of my building. I ran to see what had happened. As I got close, I saw smoke coming out of the windows of my apartment. I went crazy. I even tried to get into the building but a fireman held me back. I asked the fireman what happened and he said that the lady living below me had the stove blow up in her face. The fireman said, "Thank God you weren't home when it happened." He was right. Thank God I was alive.

I looked around and saw people making jokes and laughing like it was a show. For me, it was a nightmare to see everything I had turn into ashes. I went to a friend's house and told him what had happened. He was sorry about it but he told me I couldn't stay. That got me very upset because when I drank with him, I used to stay over sometimes. All I said was thank you and I left. I went to see some other friends. I just kept hearing the words, "Sorry, I can't let you stay." I decided not to bother anyone else.

My first night, I slept in Central Park. I went to work from there. I told my boss what had happened. I asked him for some time off to find a place to stay. He said no because he needed me to run things. So I quit.

I started to live in the streets. When it came to my family, I never heard from them again.

Living in the streets was a nightmare. I could hardly sleep because I was scared that someone would kill me or rape me. Two days later, I started to get hungry. I went to a restaurant and asked them for food. The man asked if I had money and I told him that I had only two dollars. He said that was not enough and to leave the restaurant. I didn't have any money because I paid my rent and some bills three days before my apartment got burned.

I started to lose weight and to get dirty from sleeping on rooftops and in basements. I slept behind garbage cans. Sometimes I slept on the subway trains or at the railroad station. I would go without eating or drinking for days.

You wouldn't believe how people treat you when you don't have anything. Before, people loved me. Now they treated me as if I was a nobody. In the subway, people wouldn't sit next to me and some of them would laugh and make faces. I was beginning to hate people. I spent three weeks in hell. Those three weeks felt like three years.

One day I was sitting next to a garbage can. It was really cold that day. I had my head against my knees to keep my face warm. Then I felt someone standing next to me. When I picked up my head, there was a lady looking at me. I got scared and pulled away. The lady bent down and told me not to be scared of her. Then she started to talk to me.

The next thing I knew, she opened her purse and took out five dollars, a piece of paper and a pen. She told me to take the money, get something to eat and save a dollar for carfare to a shelter. She wrote the address of a women's shelter on the paper. I asked her why she wanted to help me. She told me that she had children and that she didn't know what could happen to them in the future. She took my hand and told me to go, to get off the streets. And then she walked away.

By the time I got up to say goodbye, she was gone. I still remember her white hair and her wrinkled face. I looked at the paper again and went to eat something. Then I went on to the shelter.

PART THREE: HOW IT FEELS TO LIVE IN A SHELTER

They took me in at the shelter right away. They gave me clothes and a shower, then they took me to the room where I was going to sleep. There were ten beds in the room. I didn't say a word and went to sleep.

The next day, the workers began waking up people at 7 A.M. By 8, people had to leave the sleeping room. We were not allowed to go back there until after dinner unless you were sick.

If you didn't have a place to go, you had to sit in the TV room all day. For a few days, things were going great. I even made friends. Things changed when some other women in the shelter asked me to drink and smoke pot. They didn't like it when I said no. After that, people called me names like party pooper. I paid no attention to it.

Living in a shelter was worse than living in the streets. In the streets, you could walk away, but in the shelter, I had to see these women every day. It was another nightmare. There was prejudice—blacks against Puerto Ricans against whites—it was crazy. I wanted out. I hardly slept. People walked in their sleep and talked to themselves and there was always a fight for no reason. The place was crazy. All I wanted was to get out of there and make my life again.

Six months later, my case worker put me

to work teaching arts and crafts in the shelter. We made lamps and jewelry boxes out of ice cream sticks. The pay wasn't good but it was money in my pocket. Later I worked on the outside moving furniture from hotels to new apartments for the homeless. I liked the job because it kept me away from the shelter.

One day I received good news: I was accepted for an apartment in a new subsidized building. Around the same time, I also met a very nice girl—well, I thought she was nice. I started to see her.

Two months later, I moved out of the shelter. My new home was one room. I had to share the bathroom and the kitchen but I was happy.

PART FOUR: WHEN I GOT INTO CRACK

I was so happy the first night in my room that I cried. I was glad that my nightmare was over. I got away from the shelter. There was so much evil, so much hate. There was no privacy; people were always around you. I couldn't believe that I had put up with that shelter for eight months.

I invited the girl I liked from the shelter

to the opening of our building. She stayed for the night. The next day she came to tell me that she'd lost her bed at the shelter. I couldn't let her stay on the streets. I said she could stay over. That was my worst mistake because she started to stay every night, and little by little I fell in love.

I began to notice something funny about her. Sometimes she came in at three in the morning acting strange. It made me cold but what really got me mad was that she stole money from me. She accused someone in the building but I knew she did it.

She hung out in my neighbor's room until late at night. I decided to listen at my neighbor's door. I wanted to know what was going on. I knocked on his door but he wouldn't let me in. A few minutes later, my girlfriend let me in. I saw everything: bottles of crack, coke, pot and a pipe. She was doing crack. I couldn't believe what I was seeing.

She knew that I loved her and she played with my heart. She convinced me to try crack. I liked it. We smoked five bottles of crack the next day. When my body ached for more, I gave her 50 dollars. I got so addicted that my whole welfare check went for crack. I didn't eat so I could spend my money on crack.

I began to look like a zombie. I walked in the streets as if I were walking on a cloud. When people talked to me, I was in another world. Crack really changed me. I made fun of people. I didn't care about anyone.

One day my landlord asked to see me. I was afraid she'd found out about the crack. She told me about some volunteer work at a city agency. She thought that I was the right person for the job. She offered me a few dollars as pay plus carfare.

That night my girl and I stayed up smoking crack until three in the morning. I slept for a few hours and then went to my new job. I was to help with a clothing bank, "New Clothes for the Homeless." Clothing manufacturers and stores donated new clothing to be distributed to homeless people. My new boss took me to a small room. There were two boxes with new clothes in them. I had to inventory them. It wasn't easy because I didn't know how to read or write.

But my main problem was that I was on crack. I couldn't live without smoking. Then things started to change. I started to think how sweet I was being treated at the agency. The clothing bank started to get bigger and bigger. Almost a year later, I became a paid staff member and got off welfare. They even made me a supervisor.

That's when I decided to leave crack. I went home to talk to my girlfriend. I told her to make up her mind between me or crack because I was planning to quit. She said there was no way that she was going to stop. I told her to move out; I was not going to lose my job because of drugs. She packed up her things and left.

For the next few weeks, I locked myself in my room at night. I didn't go out for anything. My body would go crazy. I would sweat and shake. My mind imagined weird things. I had nightmares and all my dreams had to do with crack. I couldn't take it. I just wanted to kill myself.

For those weeks, I lived in pain until my body was clean. Working helped a lot because it kept my mind off crack.

I felt sorry for my girlfriend. I loved her but I knew that her love wouldn't take me anywhere. I knew I didn't have a future with her.

In time I got better. I started to eat and to

get back my weight. I came to be the person I was. Sometimes I feel that that time was a nightmare, but it was real.

PART FIVE: WHEN I FOUND MY HAPPINESS

Working with the clothing bank gave me a new life. I started to go to school to work on my reading and writing. I'm currently working toward my G.E.D. degree.

I'll always remember the day my mother and I made up: December 28, 1988. We cried together on the phone because we hadn't seen or heard from each other in ten years.

Now I live a peaceful life. I love my job and the people I work with. I've found the right companion with two beautiful children. She understands everything that I went through.

This is the happiness I have now but I don't know what could happen tomorrow. I do know I'm not afraid to face whatever comes in the future. I know how to help myself and talk to others.

Other titles in the
NEW WRITERS' VOICES series

Bars Coming Near
Stories and poems by men and women in prison.
0-929631-64-1

Never Say Good-bye
A second collection of stories and poems by men and women in prison.
1-56853-005-6

My Native Land
Essays by writers who left their native lands for America. Includes eight maps.
0-929631-65-X

When Dreams Come True
By Calvin Miles
Memories of a special childhood Christmas in South Carolina.
0-929631-18-8

Changes
Stories and poems about experiences that have shaped or reshaped the authors' lives.
1-56853-006-4

From My Imagination
Poems and short stories in a range
of genres, from science fiction to rap
to fables.
0-929631-17-X

Snapshots
Stories by new writers; one about a child's
birthday, the other about the subway.
Includes photographs.
1-56853-004-8

Speaking from the Heart
Stories and poems about love and
friendship in a variety of relationships.
0-929631-16-1

Speaking Out on Health
Personal pieces about health problems and
how the writers dealt with them.
0-929631-05-6

Speaking Out on Home and Family
Articles on many aspects of home and
family life, with photographs.
0-929631-08-0

Speaking Out on Work
Stories reflecting the authors' thoughts
about work, with photographs.
0-929631-35-8

Speaking to One Another
Pieces addressing many facets of illiteracy
from a personal point of view.
1-56853-007-2

Spending Time Together
Articles about parenting written by men,
women, and children.
1-56853-008-0

Can't Wait for Summer
By Theresa Sanseverino
Seaside adventures of a group of friends.
Includes photographs and a discussion
with the author.
0-929631-07-2

Make Way for August
By Mamie Moore
A mother's story about her daughter and
their pet guinea pig. Plus photos and a
discussion with the author.
0-929631-36-6

Fatal Beauty
By Andre Holder
An insurance detective traps a "black widow" who has lost two husbands.
1-56853-003-X

Three Shots in the Night
By Sonny Carbone
A police detective's story related by multiple characters.
0-929631-63-3

**Call 1-800-448-8878
to order books
or for a complete catalog of
Signal Hill Publications and
New Readers Press books.**